DOG

FOR DAD AND MY FIRST BOX OF CRAYONS. NL

FOR LAURA, WHO POINTED OUT THAT OUR CAT SMUDGE
THOUGHT WE WERE HER PET HUMANS - MR

Bloomsbury Publishing, London, New Delhi, New York and Sydney
First published in Great Britain in 1999 by Bloomsbury Publishing Plc
50 Bedford Square, London, WC1B 3DP

This edition first published in 2013

Text copyright © Michael Rosen 1999
Illustrations copyright © Neal Layton 1999
The moral rights of the author and illustrator have been asserted

A CIP catalogue record of this book is available from the British Library

ISBN 978 1 4088 4580 6 (PB)
ISBN 978 1 4088 3911 9 (eBook)

1 3 5 7 9 10 8 6 4 2

Printed in China by C&C Offset Printing Co Ltd, Shenzhen, Guangdong

www.bloomsbury.com

Rover

Michael Rosen Neal Layton

BLOOMSBURY

LONDON NEW DELHI NEW YORK SYDNEY

This is my pet human. Humans come in all sizes:
she's the kind who is a bit bigger than me.
I named her Rover.

Her ears are not as good as mine.
She has very weak claws.
Her coat only covers her head.

Her dad, who I call Rex, has coat on his face.
Her mum, who I call Cindy, doesn't.

Sometimes I sit on Rover. Sometimes Rover sits on Cindy.
Sometimes Rover sits on Rex.
Sometimes we all sit on each other.

Rover doesn't eat her food properly.
She pokes it with metal things.
This seems to make her
mum and dad very happy.

At night, I take Rover to her basket. It's very long and when
she's in it she hides under a cushion with small bears.

I let her have a rabbit as well,
though I would like it in my basket.

Rover's bark is very squeaky. Sometimes my friends bring over some other sma humans. As they're young we think it's all right if they bark a lot together.

When Rover and I go to the park she keeps losing her ball but I always bring it back for her.

She has to spend a lot of time watching a loud, coloured box. When she's bored with it, I wag my tail and she watches that instead.

In the summer I lead them to a bigger, family-size box and Rex
and Cindy move it very quickly to the seaside.
I help it go faster by putting my head out of the window.

We go to an enormous sandpit where the humans rip off nearly all their winter overclothes. Then some of them run about in coloured underclothes, and some lie down and pretend to be dead.

One day last summer we sat in the sandpit while the wind
blew the sand all over us. I liked it but Rex and Cindy didn't.
In the end they fell asleep under a blanket.

Near where we were sitting, a man and woman were trying to eat each other.
That was when Rover went for a walk.
I was sad to see her getting smaller and smaller and then disappear.

Then Rex came out from under his blanket.
He stood up and looked up and down the sandpit.
Then he woke up Cindy and they
both started barking.

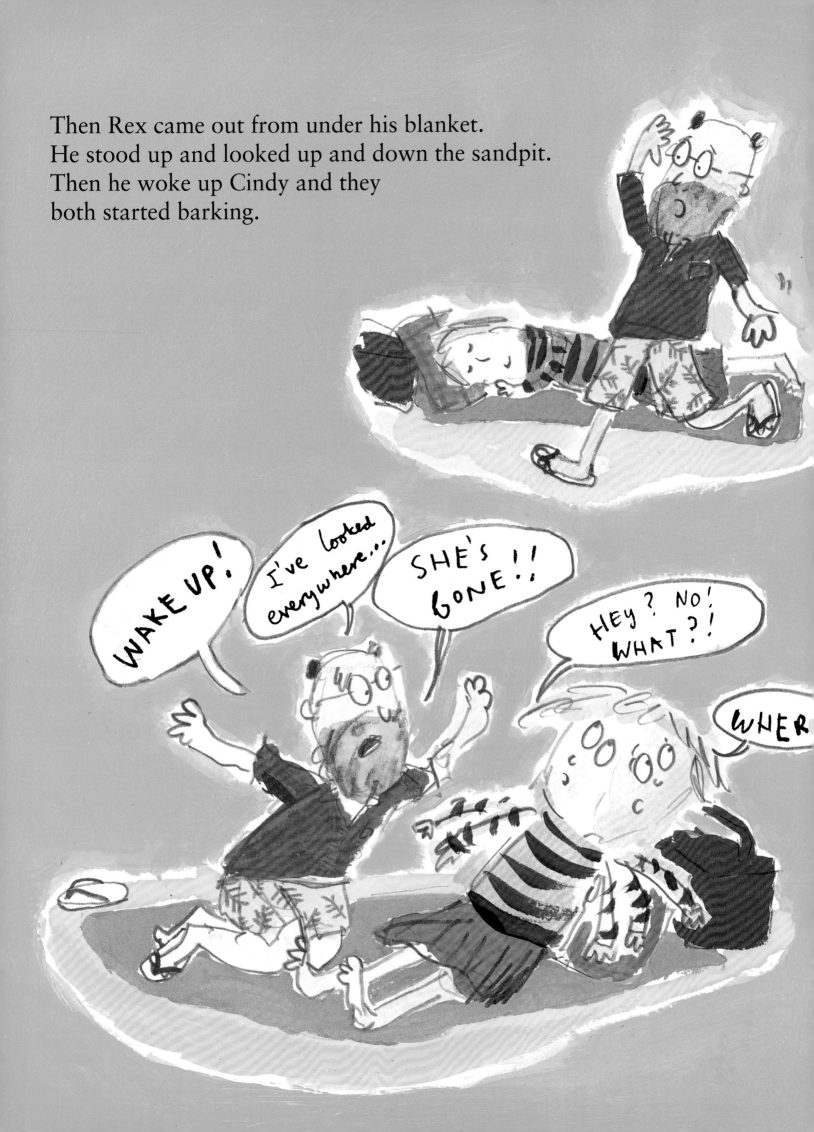

Cindy rushed over to the people eating each other
and started pointing all over the sandpit and barking some more.
Then they all looked at me.

Rex waved Rover's rabbit under my nose and barked at me.
It was getting very loud and all the people who had been lying down
now stood up. Cindy patted me and Rex waved Rover's rabbit again.

I thought it was time to go back to the box but I didn't want
to go without Rover. So, I walked off down the sandpit to fetch her.

Rex and Cindy walked behind me. They kept looking at the sea. Every human we walked past they barked at.

There was a group of humans who were trying to smash a ball into a net. Sometimes they missed and it went over. Then they barked a lot.

I couldn't see Rover.

Rex and Cindy were breathing loudly and there were
more lines on their faces than usual.

Then we got to the rocks.
In between the rocks there were puddles.

In the puddles there were
funny-looking things with
eight legs that walked sideways.

Rex and Cindy wanted to go back and tried to make me come too. I thought that was a bad idea because as far as I knew we had come to the rocks to get Rover and bring her back.

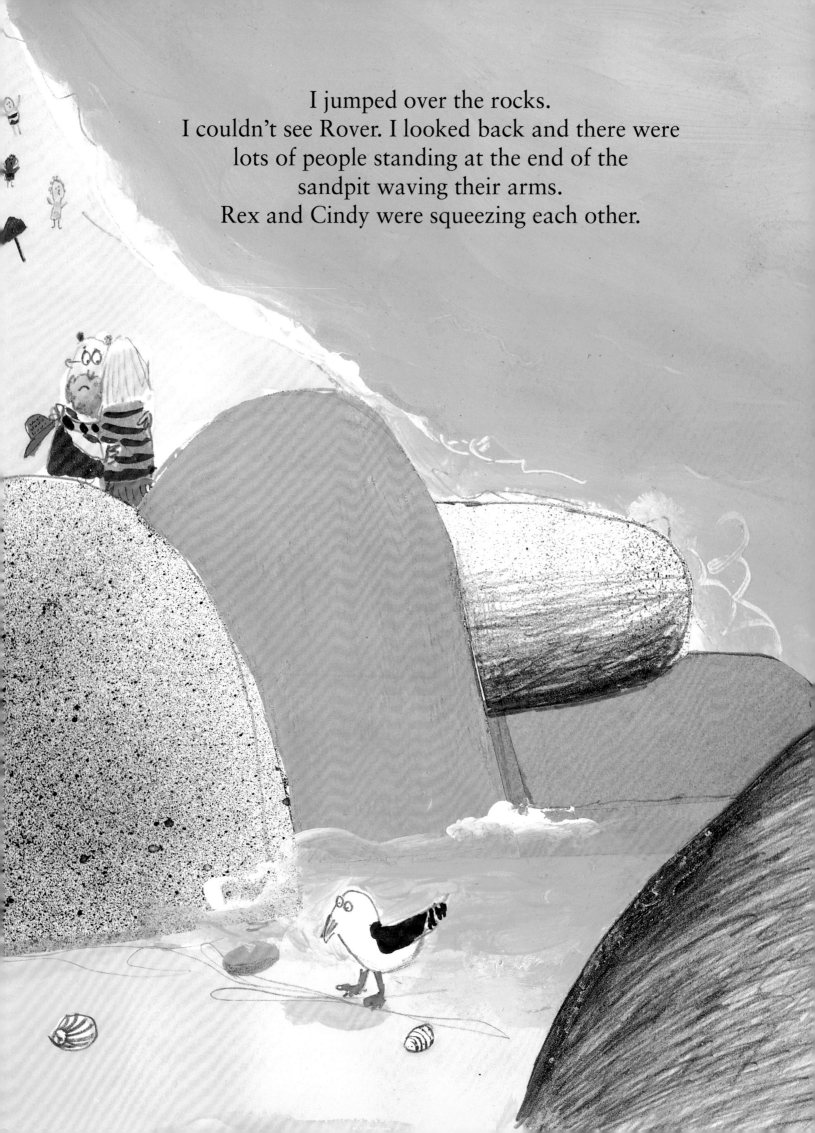

I jumped over the rocks.
I couldn't see Rover. I looked back and there were
lots of people standing at the end of the
sandpit waving their arms.
Rex and Cindy were squeezing each other.

Then I jumped over one more rock and there was Rover staring into a puddle.

I barked. She looked at me and pointed at one of the funny
eight-legged things. I barked again, and Rex and Cindy came
over the top of the rock and started barking and howling.
Their eyes were all watery and they rushed up to
Rover and picked her up and squeezed her.

Then we headed back. Cindy and Rex kept patting me
all over and squeezed my neck. Quite a lot.
Rex kept showing Rover's rabbit to everyone and pointing at me.

At last we could all get
in the box and go home.

And I thought: next time Rover starts getting smaller and smaller,
I'll chase after her to keep her nice and big.
It will save a lot of fuss.